MW00932296

Kenna, the very Scottish dog, lives with her

very Scottish mom, Annette.

Kenna loves spending cozy time with Annette.

On the days Annette must go to work,

Kenna is home alone. Being home by herself

makes Kenna feel lonely.

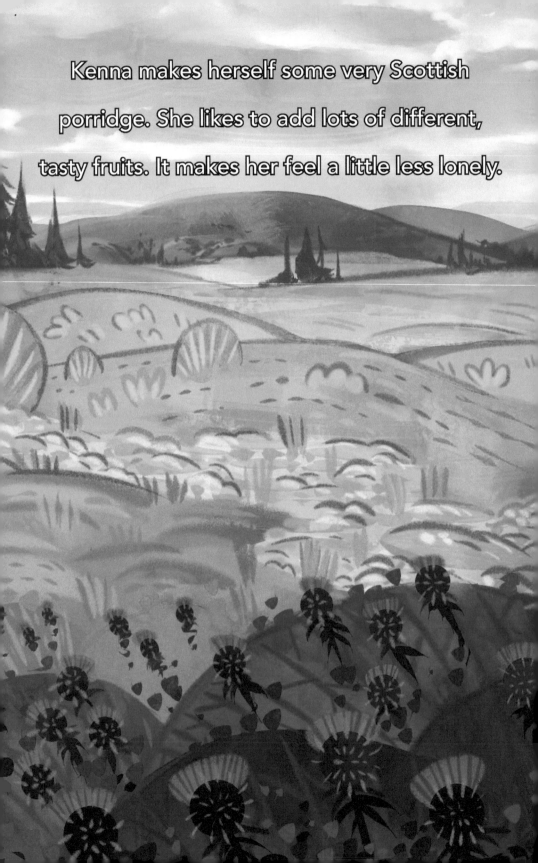

Kenna makes herself some very Scottish porridge. She likes to add lots of different, tasty fruits. It makes her feel a little less lonely.

# Kenna

## the Very Scottish Dog

### By Sarah E. Paul
### Illustrated by Tara Lehning

# Acknowledgements:

I would like to thank my friends and family once again for their valuable contributions to the final version of this story. To list everyone would likely be impossible, but you know who you are… you're the best!

Thank you to Nick and Holly for editing.

Thank you to Kristi for the layout and graphic design.

Thank you to Tara, who once again, has elevated the story to a whole new level with her incredible art.

Thank you to my aunt and uncle and our shared affinity for Scottish things.

Copyright © 2022 Sarah E. Paul
ISBN 978-1-38754-714-2
All rights reserved.
Printed in the U.S.A.

This edition's first printing was October 2022

Edited by Nick Turner
Edited by Holly Meehleis
Layout by Tara Lehning and Kristi Siedow-Thompson
Graphic design by Kristi Siedow-Thompson

For my mom,
who always let me pursue
every single interest.


And for Uncle David, Aunt Annette,
and their late dog Kenna,
who inspired this story.

Kenna tends to her garden and smells her very Scottish thistles. She loves the purple color. It makes her feel a little less lonely.

Kenna decides to visit her

very Scottish friend, Nessie.

She loves to play with Nessie.

It makes her feel a little less lonely.

Kenna puts on her very Scottish tartan skirt

with a matching bow.

She likes to dress up to see her friends.

Kenna likes to walk along the path

to Nessie's very Scottish loch.

Nessie is very happy to see her friend.


"I am glad to see you, Kenna!"

"I am SO glad to see you, Nessie!"


Nessie hugs her friend Kenna and invites her

to go for a swim in her very Scottish loch.

When Nessie and Kenna go for a swim,
Nessie lets Kenna ride on her back.

They wave at some very Scottish gray seals
and bottlenose dolphins.

Kenna loves to play water games in the loch
with her friends.

When they are finished swimming,
Nessie tells Kenna about the very Scottish
Highland Games that are happening today.
Kenna can't wait to see all the events with her
friend Nessie.

At the Highland Games,

Kenna and Nessie see their friend Fergus.

He is about to play

the very Scottish caber toss game.

Kenna and Nessie take a seat in the stands
and cheer for their friend Fergus.
Kenna loves to cheer for her friends.

"Go, Fergus! Go!"

Fergus tosses the caber SO HIGH.

Fergus has turned the caber! He did it!

Kenna and Nessie cheer louder.

"WOOOOO! FERGUS!"

Fergus asks if his friends would like to learn some highland games. He teaches Nessie the very Scottish sheaf toss. Nessie tosses the sheaf SO FAR. She did it!

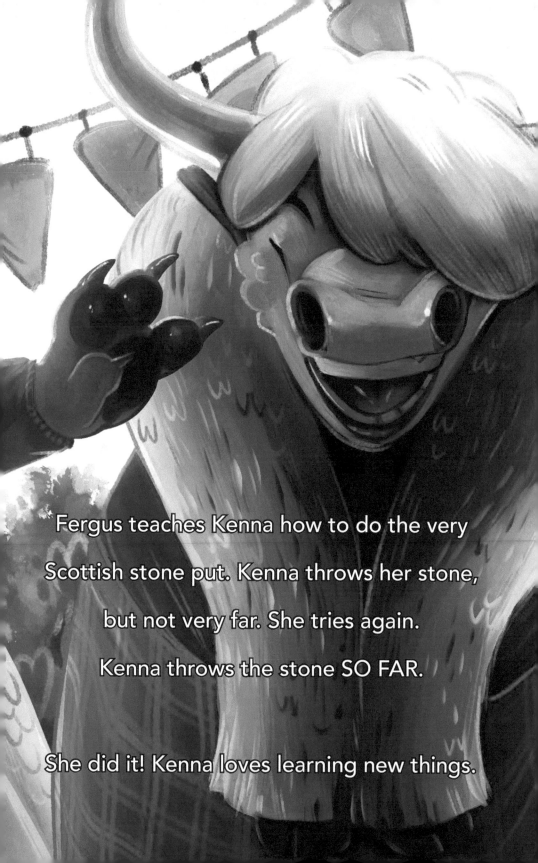

Fergus teaches Kenna how to do the very
Scottish stone put. Kenna throws her stone,
but not very far. She tries again.
Kenna throws the stone SO FAR.

She did it! Kenna loves learning new things.

After all the fun at the Highland Games, the friends join in some very Scottish step dancing to some very Scottish bagpipes.

Kenna loves dancing with her friends.

Kenna asks her friends to have some
very Scottish lunch.

The friends try some very Scottish haggis
with some very Scottish neeps and tatties.

Fergus does not like haggis,
but he likes the neeps and tatties!

Kenna loves eating food with her friends.

Fergus says goodbye to his friends.

"Thank you for all the fun!" he says,

and he heads home.

Kenna and Nessie say goodbye
and walk back to Nessie's loch.

Kenna hugs her friend Nessie and waves goodbye as Nessie swims back home. Kenna walks home and thinks of all the fun she had during her very Scottish day.

She is not feeling lonely anymore.

Kenna gets home and sits on her favorite couch. Annette comes home to greet her very Scottish daughter.

"Hello, Kenna! How was your day?"

"I was feeling lonely, but then I decided to do all my favorite things," says Kenna.

"It's not lonely when you do your favorite things. I'm glad I'm home to hear all about it," says Annette.

Annette fixes dinner and Kenna, the very Scottish dog, shares her very Scottish day with her very Scottish mom.

The End

# Some Very Scottish Words:

Bagpipes – A very loud instrument

Caber – A very big wooden pole

Haggis – A traditional meat dish

Loch – An inlet of seawater

Neeps and Tatties – Mashed turnips and potatoes

Tartan – A cloth with a colorful criss cross pattern

Thistle – A flowering, prickly plant

## About the Author

**Sarah E. Paul** is a children's author, actress, vocalist, cosplayer, wife, and an all-around humorous individual. She enjoys comic books, roller-skating and playing with her dogs and her pet bird. Kenna is her second book after *I Wish I Were A Superhero*. Sarah hopes to write many more stories in the future. She hopes her stories inspire kindness and strength.

## About the Illustrator

**Tara Lehning** is a creature concept artist who works in the digital 2D medium and in digital 3D. She enjoys creating biologically and evolutionarily accurate animals tailored to a specific environment. She prefers to paint these creatures existing within their world because they seem more believable and concrete, performing speculative behaviors as a real animal might. She wants to be a part of the incredible worlds that development teams bring to life.

CPSIA information can be obtained
at www.ICGtesting.com
Printed in the USA
BVHW021905081122
651457BV00001B/5